I AM HENRY FINCH

For Ben Norland

First published in 2014 by Walker Books Ltd, 87 Vauxhall Walk, London SE11 5HJ

10 9 8 7 6 5 4 3 2 1

Text © 2014 Alexis Deacon • Illustrations © 2014 Viviane Schwarz

This book has been typeset in Helvetica Neue

Printed in China

British Library Cataloguing in Publication Data: a catalogue record for this book is available from the British Library

ISBN 978-1-4063-5713-4

www.walker.co.uk

I Am Henry Finch

Alexis Deacon   illustrated by Viviane Schwarz

WALKER BOOKS
AND SUBSIDIARIES

LONDON • BOSTON • SYDNEY • AUCKLAND

The finches lived in a great flock.
They made such a racket all day long, you
really could not hear yourself think.

Every morning they said, GOOD MORNING.

Every afternoon they said, GOOD AFTERNOON.

In the evening they said, GOOD EVENING.

At night they said, GOOD NIGHT.

In the morning they started over.

It was always the same.
Except ...

sometimes the Beast came.

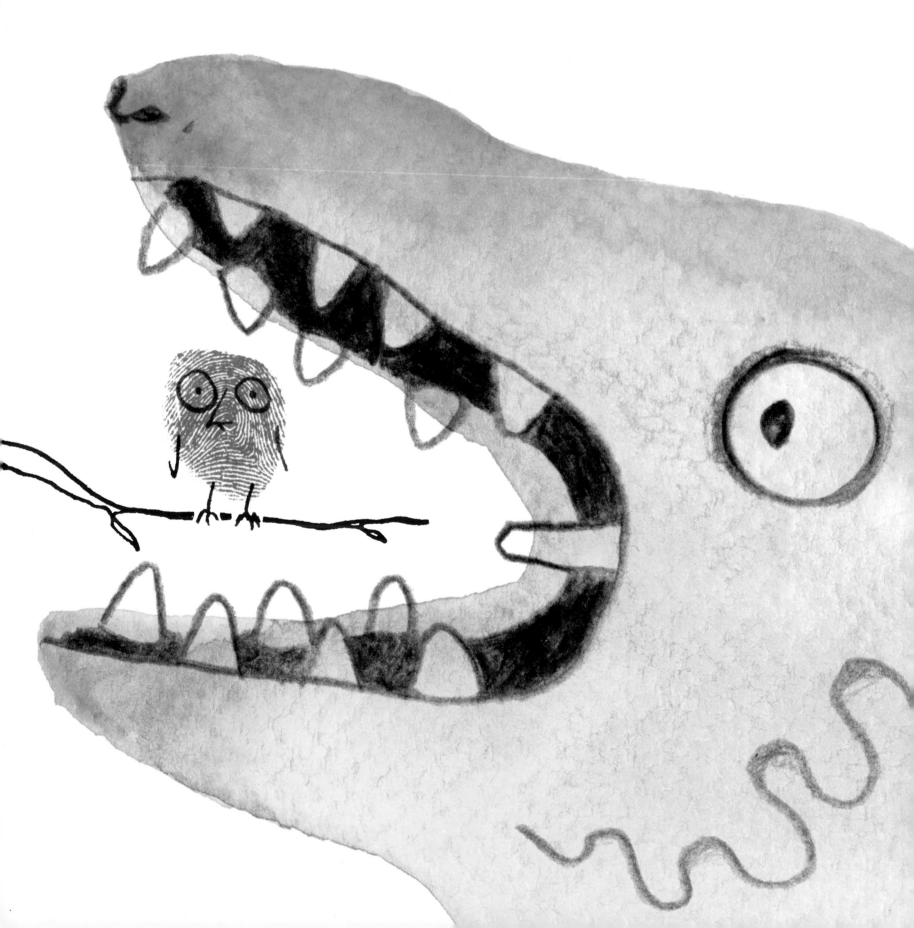

Then they would all shout,
THE BEAST, THE BEAST...

and fly as fast as they could
to the top of the nearest tree,
where they would sit and shout
until the Beast moved on.

This was the way it always was.

Until ...

one night ...

something else ...

happened.

A finch woke up in the dark
and the quiet.

He had a thought and he heard it.

I AM HENRY FINCH,

he thought.

I THINK,

he thought.

He sat still and listened to his thoughts.

He had more of them.

He liked them.

AM I THE FIRST FINCH TO EVER HAVE A THOUGHT? he thought.

I COULD
BE GREAT,
thought Henry.

The next morning the Beast came.

It was the time for greatness.

I AM HENRY FINCH!

screamed Henry Finch and dived
down straight at the Beast …

who ate him.

It was very dark inside
the Beast and very quiet.

I WILL LISTEN TO MY THOUGHTS,
Henry Finch said.

But they were bad thoughts.

YOU ARE A FOOL, HENRY FINCH,
he thought.

YOU ARE NOT GREAT. YOU ARE
ONLY SOMEONE'S DINNER.

Now Henry did not like his
thoughts at all. He tried not to think,
but what else could he do?

He thought and thought and thought.

WHO AM I? he thought.
AM I HENRY FINCH?
I AM SOMETHING, I THINK.

I AM,
he thought.

IT IS,

he thought.

He became aware of
the sounds around him.

CRUNCH

MUNCH

They were the sounds
of the Beast.

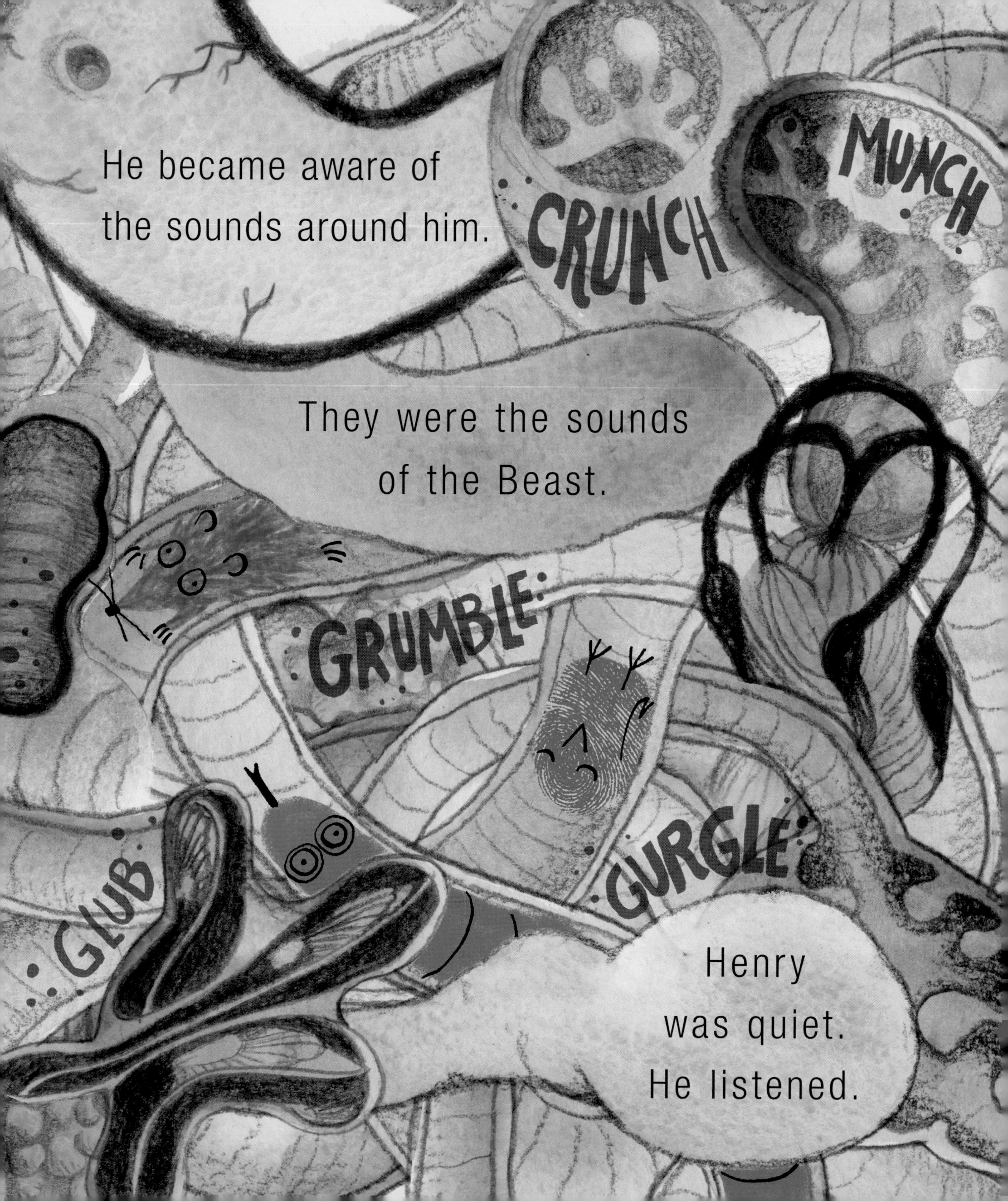

GRUMBLE

GLUB

GURGLE

Henry
was quiet.
He listened.

He could hear the thoughts of the Beast!

GOT TO EAT.
GOT TO HUNT. GOT TO
FIND MORE FOOD.
BIG FAMILY ALL NEED
FEEDING. CRAWLING,
SWIMMING, FLYING,
WALKING ... ANYTHING
WILL DO.

NO!

said Henry.

NO? thought the Beast.

THOSE CREATURES HAVE FAMILIES LIKE YOU, said Henry.

LIKE ME? thought the Beast.

YOU WILL EAT PLANTS FROM NOW ON, said Henry. THEY HAVE BITS TO SPARE.

I WILL EAT PLANTS, thought the Beast.

AND NOW, said Henry. YOU WILL OPEN YOUR MOUTH AS WIDE AS YOU CAN AND HOLD IT LIKE THAT FOR A BIT.

OPEN,

thought the beast.

Out flew Henry!

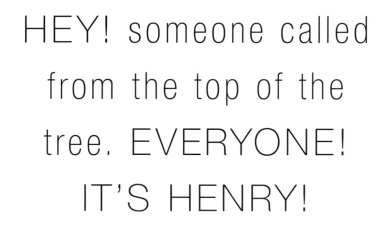

HEY! someone called
from the top of the
tree. EVERYONE!
IT'S HENRY!

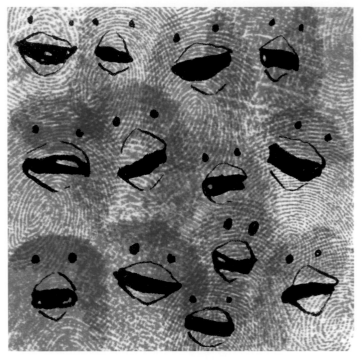

GOOD MORNING,
EVERYONE, said Henry.

GOOD MORNING, HENRY
FINCH, said everyone.

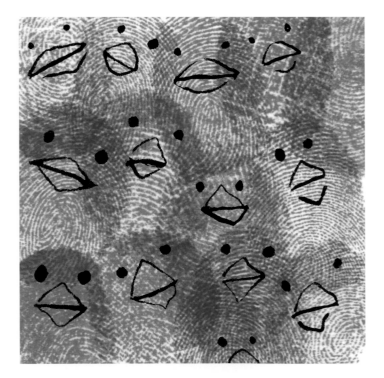

I HAVE SOMETHING TO TELL
YOU, said Henry. BUT FIRST
YOU HAVE TO BE QUIET.

Everyone was quiet.

Henry told the finches about everything
that had happened and they listened.

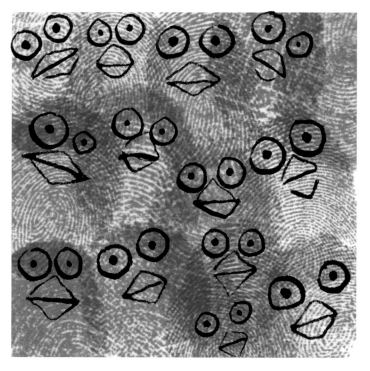

When he had finished no one
moved. They stayed quiet.

Then a little voice said,

I HAVE HAD A THOUGHT.
GOODBYE, EVERYONE.
I WILL COME BACK.

One by one the finches flew off.
WE WILL COME BACK,
they called behind them.

Henry looked up at them.
He smiled a finch smile.

GREAT,

thought Henry.

MARK EZRA

The Prickly Hedgehog

Pictures by GAVIN ROWE

Magi Publications, London

It was Little Hedgehog's first day out.
His mother was leading a food hunt,
and he hurried along behind his four prickly
brothers and sisters as fast as his short legs
could carry him. But it was no good.
In no time at all he was left way behind.

A big butterfly landed on Little Hedgehog's
snout. He tried to brush it off, but it fluttered
away over his head and he overbalanced.
By the time he had picked himself up,
his family had completely disappeared.

"They can't have gone far," thought
Little Hedgehog, pulling off all the dry
leaves that were stuck to his coat.
"That feels better," he said, as he set off to
look for them.

Oh good, there they were in the clearing ahead!
Little Hedgehog grunted with joy.
He scuttled forward, but all he
found was . . .

. . . a circle of hedgehog mushrooms
with little spines poking out from
under their caps.
"Mm, these look good to eat," he said,
and he stuck four of them on his back.
"But where *are* my family?" he wondered
very sadly.

Ah, there they were, at the foot
of that hedge! Little Hedgehog's
eyes lit up and his heart beat faster.
But when he got there, all he found
was a broken teasel twig with some
teasels on it.

"Wrong again!" said Little Hedgehog.
He ran on, and bumped into a big tree.
"How tall it is!" he said, looking upwards.
"But what's that up there?"

High up on a branch Little
Hedgehog thought he saw his
family. It seemed an awfully long
way to climb, but some ivy grew up
the tree and it gave him
a foothold.

Twig by twig and branch by branch
he climbed up through the leaves.
He teetered along a thin bough
towards the spiny little group.
He had never been so scared in
his life, but he knew he must be
brave and not look down.

When he reached them,
Little Hedgehog saw that
his climb was in vain.
"Stupid me!" he exclaimed,
for they were only a bunch
of spiny chestnuts.

He reached out and stuck four on
his back. It wasn't easy, and when he
turned round he lost his balance
and fell . . .

. . . and as he fell down and down, he curled into a tight ball and bounced onto a soft bed of leaves. "Bother!" said Little Hedgehog, wriggling round to pull the leaves from his spiny back.

Suddenly Little Hedgehog heard a loud
noise, and an enormous creature bounded
up to him. He didn't know it was a
friendly dog. He was absolutely terrified.
Once again, he curled right up into a
tight ball to protect himself.

Moments passed.
Had the creature gone?
Little Hedgehog uncurled,
and to his horror he saw the
dog's big head bending
down towards him . . .

The dog picked him up in his powerful jaws,
and trotted along the path with him.
Then, just as suddenly, he dropped him.
The frightened little hedgehog landed on
a soft mossy bank.

Little Hedgehog stayed curled
up for a long time.
He was still very frightened.
Then suddenly he heard some
familiar snorting sounds.
He opened his eyes . . .

. . . and there was his mother
and his brothers and sisters!
"Where have you been?"
asked his mother.

Little Hedgehog uncurled
himself.
"Oh, just hunting for food,"
he said. "See what I've brought
back for you!"

His mother looked at the feast of food
on Little Hedgehog's back.
"Mushrooms and chestnuts!" cried all his
brothers and sisters. They all tucked
in till their tummies were quite full.
Then they fell asleep under their
favourite hedge.

Little Hedgehog's mother licked his face clean, and found him some ripe berries. The prickly little hedgehog never told his mother all about his adventures, but I think she must have guessed.
Don't you?

For Arabella

LONDON BOROUGH OF WANDSWORTH	
9030 00006 1927 4	
Askews & Holts	20-Sep-2018
JF	£11.99
	WW18008265

First published 2018 by Nosy Crow Ltd
The Crow's Nest, 14 Baden Place, Crosby Row
London SE1 1YW
www.nosycrow.com

ISBN 978 1 78800 271 4

Nosy Crow and associated logos are trademarks
and/or registered trademarks of Nosy Crow Ltd.

Text and illustrations © Nicola O'Byrne 2018

The right of Nicola O'Byrne to be identified as the author
and the illustrator of this work has been asserted.

A CIP catalogue record for this book is available from the British Library.

Printed in China

Papers used by Nosy Crow are made from wood grown in sustainable forests.

10 9 8 7 6 5 4 3 2 1

The Rabbit,  THE DARK  and the Biscuit Tin

By Nicola O'Byrne

 nosy crow

Once upon a time,
there was a rabbit who
didn't want to go to sleep.

Rabbit was in his garden
when it started to get dark.
"Bother!" squeaked Rabbit. "I'm not
tired and I don't want to go to bed!"

Then a bright idea popped
into his head.

"I don't want to go to bed,"
said Rabbit, "and if it doesn't
get dark, I won't have to."

So Rabbit found his best biscuit tin.
There was **just one** biscuit left . . .

and then he went outside to find The Dark.

The Dark was not hard to find.

"Excuse me, would you like
a biscuit?" asked Rabbit.

"Don't mind if I do!"
said The Dark . . .

SNAP!

. . .

Rabbit trapped The Dark
in the biscuit tin . . .

and sat on it.

"That wasn't very polite, Rabbit,"
said The Dark from inside the tin.

"I'm sorry, but I'm not tired and
I don't want to go to bed!" said Rabbit.
"Now I can stay up all night long
because it's not dark."

"But many animals need me," said The Dark.
"They don't like the sun. When you're getting
ready for bed, they're just getting up."

"But who?" asked Rabbit.

"US!"
squeaked the bats.

"US!"
hooted the owls.

"US!"
whispered the fox cubs.

"I don't care,"
said Rabbit . . .

. . . and he took the tin back inside.

"Please let me out of the tin.
The animals need me," said The Dark.

"No. I'm not tired and I don't
want to go to bed! And it's not dark
so I don't have to," said Rabbit.

"But . . . I am a bit hungry."

BISCUITS

"What about having some breakfast?"
said The Dark. "It's your favourite meal
of the day. But you can't eat breakfast
unless you've gone to bed."

"Oh," said Rabbit. "I do
like toast and honey
and fresh orange juice.

But . . .

Actually, I like carrots most of all.
And I can eat carrots any time."

"If you let me out of the tin,
you can have carrots
AND toast
AND honey
AND fresh orange juice,"
said The Dark.

"I don't care," said Rabbit,
"and I won't go to bed!"

"Are you getting grumpy, Rabbit?"
said The Dark.

"No, I am **not**," said Rabbit,
grumpily.

"I think you are," said The Dark.
"That's what happens when
people don't go to sleep."

"I'm NOT TIRED!" said Rabbit
and stormed back out into the garden.

The garden was hot.
Rabbit was hot.
Everything was too hot.

"Oh no! My carrots!
They're wilting," said Rabbit.
"What shall I do?"

"See?" said The Dark.
"Carrots need me too."

"What?" asked Rabbit.

"Bedtime," said The Dark.
"And bedtime stories.

Once upon a time, there was a rabbit
who didn't want to go to sleep . . ."

And soon enough,

Rabbit was fast asleep.